For Binni Mao (aka Rida Khan)
—M. A. F.

To shoe girls, Auntie Te, Kathy, and Mary
—E. Y.

Text copyright © 2008 by Musharraf Ali Farooqi
Illustrations copyright © 2008 by Eugene Yelchin
A Neal Porter Book
Published by Roaring Brook Press
Roaring Brook Press is a division of Holtzbrinck Publishing Holdings Limited
Partnership
175 Fifth Avenue, New York, New York 10010
All rights reserved
www.roaringbrookpress.com

Distributed in Canada by H. B. Fenn and Company, Ltd.

Library of Congress Cataloging-in-Publication Data
Farooqi, Musharraf, 1968–
The cobbler's holiday, or why ants don't wear shoes / Musharraf Farooqi ;
illustrated by Eugene Yelchin. — 1st ed.
p. cm.
"A Neal Porter book."
Summary: At a time when every ant has at least fifteen pairs of shoes
and disputes over footwear are common, the one and only ant cobbler
decides to take some time off, which leads to many tears until the
Red Ant provides an elegant solution.
ISBN-13: 978-1-59643-234-5   ISBN-10: 1-59643-234-9
[1. Shoes—Fiction.   2. Ants—Fiction.   3. Fashion—Fiction.] I. Yelchin, Eugene, ill.
II. Title.   III. Title: Cobbler's holiday.   IV. Title: Why ants don't wear shoes.
V. Title: Why ants do not wear shoes.
PZ7.F2393Cob 2008   [E]—dc22   2007044046

Roaring Brook Press books are available for special promotions and premiums.
For details contact: Director of Special Markets, Holtzbrinck Publishers.

Printed in China
Book design by Barbara Grzeslo
First edition September 2008
1 3 5 7 9 10 8 6 4 2

THE
COBBLER'S HOLIDAY
OR
WHY ANTS DON'T WEAR SHOES

MUSHARRAF ALI FAROOQI Illustrated by EUGENE YELCHIN

A NEAL PORTER BOOK ✒ ROARING BROOK PRESS 👞 NEW YORK

he closets in ants' houses were once full of shoes. As each had six feet, an ant needed three pairs of shoes for each occasion—three pairs for work, three pairs for outdoors, three pairs for play, three pairs for parties, and three pairs of slippers. Fifteen pairs in all. In short, thirty shoes. And all this for one ant alone.

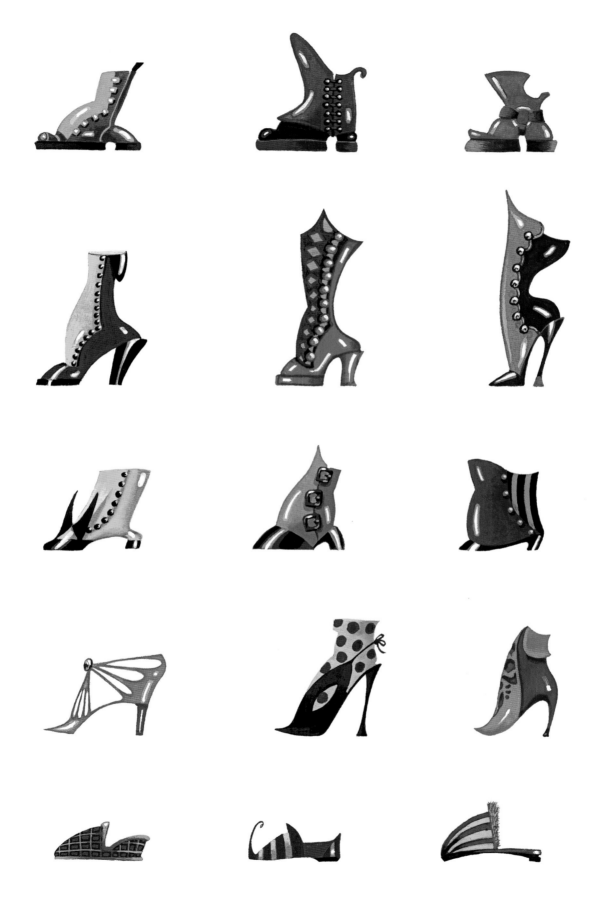

nts did not wear three identical pairs, unless they were soldiers. It was often a case of "mix and match," although the lady ants liked to wear shoes that went with different outfits. There were so many kinds of shoes that the entrance halls of ants' houses were always piled high with them.

 t ant parties, guests arrived wearing three pairs of outdoor shoes and carrying another three pairs of party shoes to be changed at the door. As a result, guests would invariably lose some of their shoes.

The after-party shoe searches were the biggest cause of disputes among ants. And since others might be wearing shoes of the same kind, guests often mistook somebody else's for their own.

ome dishonest ants had made it a practice to go to parties wearing old shoes and return wearing new ones, taking advantage of the chaos.

Sometimes scuffles broke out between the guests if someone was found putting on somebody else's shoes. In these clashes, shoes were convenient weapons.

As ants are very busy creatures, half of their day was spent running errands. The other half was taken up by their favorite dance, the Tick-Toe-Hip-Clog-Tock-Hop. It required thirty-six hundred steps in all for a pair to make a full turn. Of course, nobody ever completed a half turn without forgetting a step. But then the ants always thought it amusing to begin things all over again.

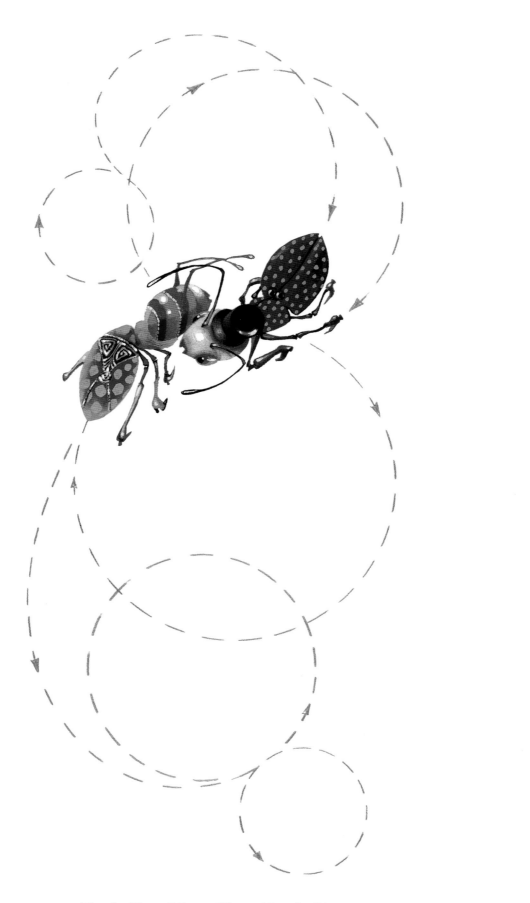

Tick-Toe-Hip-Clog-Tock-Hop

ecause of the ants' many activities, their shoes were subject to much wear and tear. But there was only one cobbler ant among all of them. And since he was needed at all hours, and did all the work by himself, his shop never closed. Some days would be spent mending shoes, others designing new ones, sometimes cutting leather and other times stitching—all with his mouth, of course. He always had plenty of work. And all that hard work had made him very rich.

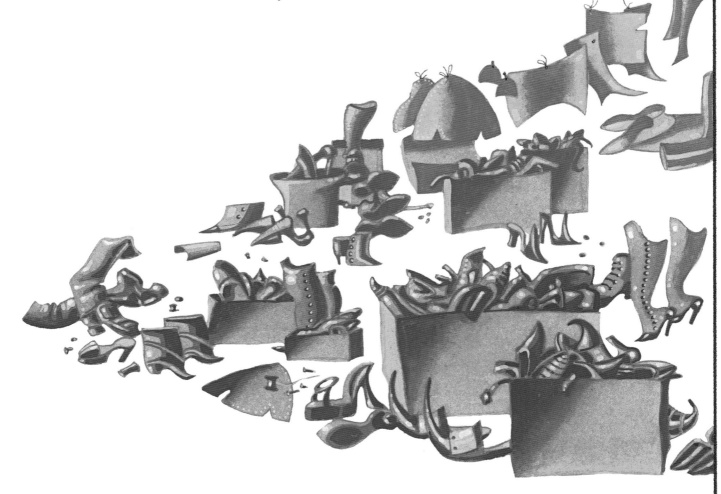

hile sewing a shoe one day, he accidentally bit his foot. Such a thing had never happened before. "I must be working too hard!" he said, and decided to take a vacation.

he next morning, the cobbler's customers found the shop closed. "What could this mean?" they asked each other. Nobody knew the answer, as the shop had never closed before. "We will ask the cobbler when he returns!" they said, and rushed away, as they were getting late for their errands.

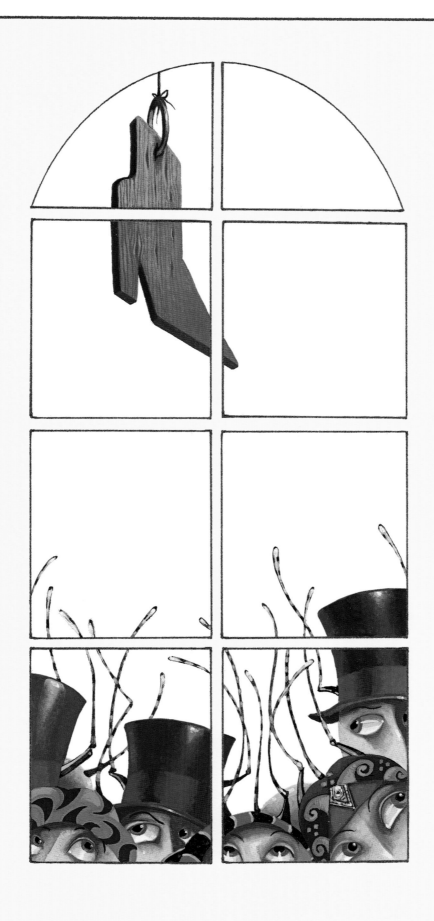

 day's rest did wonders for the cobbler ant. He enjoyed it very much. "Why on earth was I working so hard?" he wondered. He checked his bank account and found that he had enough money never to work again. He decided to spend the rest of his life traveling. He packed all his money in a bag and went away without telling anyone.

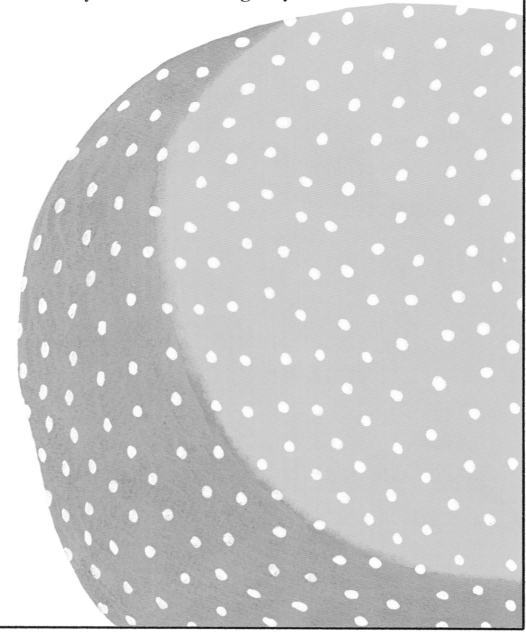

he next day when the ants found the shop closed again, they went searching for the cobbler, but he could not be found. Day followed day, one after another. The cobbler was never seen again, nor did his shop reopen. Shoes with broken straps, worn-out soles, and broken heels began piling up at an alarming rate.

"How irresponsible of the cobbler!" said the ants who were stylish, after a week had passed. They felt the cobbler's absence the most. It greatly distressed them that there was nobody to make new shoes. They did not wish to be seen wearing the same pair of shoes twice.

ome more days passed, and from their constant walking and dancing, the ants wore out all the heels of all their shoes. Then the stylish ants were forced to declare that it was all right to wear shoes without heels and that no great harm would come from wearing the same pair again. This reassured the others, and for the time being, they forgot all about the problem.

But the ants kept walking and dancing, and the soles of their shoes wore out next. Now when they walked, they dragged their shoes. Frantic searches were again made for the cobbler, and again he failed to turn up. The stylish ants dragged their feet to the parties and bumbled and stumbled at every step because of the long dresses they wore to cover up their old shoes. They found it impossible, under the circumstances, to dance the Tick-Toe-Hip-Clog-Tock-Hop with any grace.

ne evening while the ants were attending a party shedding bitter tears at their misfortune, the door opened and the Red Ant walked in barefoot. There was not a single shoe on any of her feet.

"What a scandal!" cried one of the fashionable old-timers. The other guests were also shocked at the sight of her gliding about the room barefoot.

ut the barefoot Red Ant was a marvel to watch when it was time to dance the Tick-Toe-Hip-Clog-Tock-Hop. What poise! What grace! In fact, she came very near to completing a full turn. One by one, other guests began flinging off their shoes too—despite objections from the fashionable ants. And they immediately felt lighter and more relaxed. They felt nimble. They found that barefoot, they could dance with perfect grace.

he stylish ants decided to remain silent forever about what had happened that evening. But the word spread.

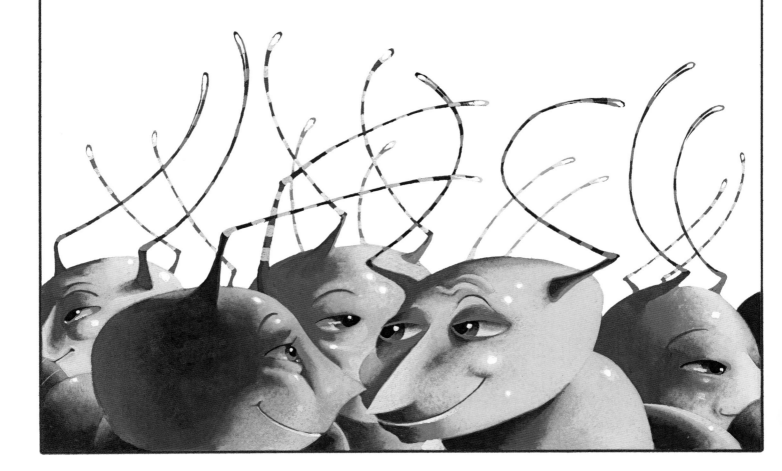

The party had been a great success, and at the end there were no fights as no one had any shoes to collect.

Later, the Red Ant was invited to many parties. Everywhere she went, she declared walking barefoot to be healthy, fashionable, and wise. Suddenly, she became the *most* stylish ant around town. More and more ants appeared barefoot in public. And finally a day came when all the stylish ants gave up shoes too, fearing that they might be called old-fashioned. And from that day to this, all ants have walked barefoot.